"We all have our time machines, don't we. Those that take us back are memories...And those that carry us forward, are dreams."

H.G. Wells - The Time Machine

Ruyton XI Towns
A Village Rich in History and Character

Nestled in the heart of Shropshire, England, lies the village of Ruyton XI Towns, a place steeped in history and brimming with picturesque charm. This village, with its unique name and storied past, offers a fascinating glimpse into the tapestry of English rural life, marked by historical significance, geographical beauty, and a community spirit that has endured through the ages.

Historical Background

Ruyton XI Towns derives its unusual name from a historical anomaly. Originally named simply Ruyton, the suffix "XI Towns" was added to denote the village's status as a central hub for eleven surrounding townships. These included Coton, Eardiston, Felton, Haughton, Rednal, Shelvock, Shotatton, Sutton, Tedsmore, Weirbrook, and Wykey.

This configuration likely dates back to the medieval period when Ruyton served as an administrative and judicial center for these communities.

The village's history is marked by several significant events. In the 12th century, the de Ruyton family established Ruyton Castle, although today, little remains of the original structure. The castle's remnants, however, hint at its former grandeur and its role in the defense of the region. During the English Civil War, the area was a site of minor skirmishes, reflecting the broader national conflict between Royalists and Parliamentarians.

Geography and Landscape

Ruyton XI Towns is situated in a scenic part of Shropshire, characterized by rolling hills, lush meadows, and the meandering River Perry, which flows through the village.

This river not only enhances the village's aesthetic appeal but also played a crucial role in its historical development, providing water for agriculture and serving as a natural boundary.

The village is located approximately 10 miles northwest of Shrewsbury, the county town of Shropshire, and is easily accessible via the A5 road. This proximity to Shrewsbury ensures that Ruyton XI Towns benefits from the amenities of a larger town while retaining its tranquil, rural character.

The landscape around Ruyton XI Towns is quintessentially English, with a patchwork of farmland, woodlands, and quaint cottages. The area is ideal for outdoor enthusiasts, offering numerous walking and cycling routes that showcase the natural beauty of the Shropshire countryside

Community and Culture

Ruyton XI Towns is a vibrant community with a population of around 1,500 residents. Despite its small size, the village boasts a range of amenities, including a primary school, a village hall, and several local businesses. The community is known for its strong sense of identity and active participation in local events and initiatives.

One of the village's most notable cultural landmarks is St. John the Baptist Church. This Grade II listed building dates back to the 12th century and features stunning architectural details, including a Norman doorway and a medieval tower. The church remains a focal point for community gatherings and religious services. The village also hosts an array of annual events that bring residents together and attract visitors from surrounding areas.

These include the Ruyton XI Towns Carnival, a lively celebration featuring parades, games, and local crafts, as well as various seasonal fairs and markets that showcase the talents and products of local artisans.

Modern Developments

In recent years, Ruyton XI Towns has seen several developments aimed at preserving its historical heritage while accommodating modern needs. Efforts to maintain and restore historical buildings have been complemented by initiatives to improve infrastructure and community facilities. The village hall, for instance, has been refurbished to better serve as a venue for social, educational, and recreational activities. Furthermore, Ruyton XI Towns has embraced sustainability with projects designed to protect the environment and promote green living. Community gardens, recycling programs, and conservation efforts are all part of the village's commitment to a sustainable future.

Conclusion

Ruyton XI Towns is a village that beautifully blends historical significance with contemporary vibrancy. Its unique name reflects a rich past, while its scenic geography and strong community spirit make it a delightful place to live and visit. Whether exploring its historical landmarks, enjoying the natural landscape, or participating in local events, Ruyton XI Towns offers a quintessentially English experience that captivates all who encounter it.

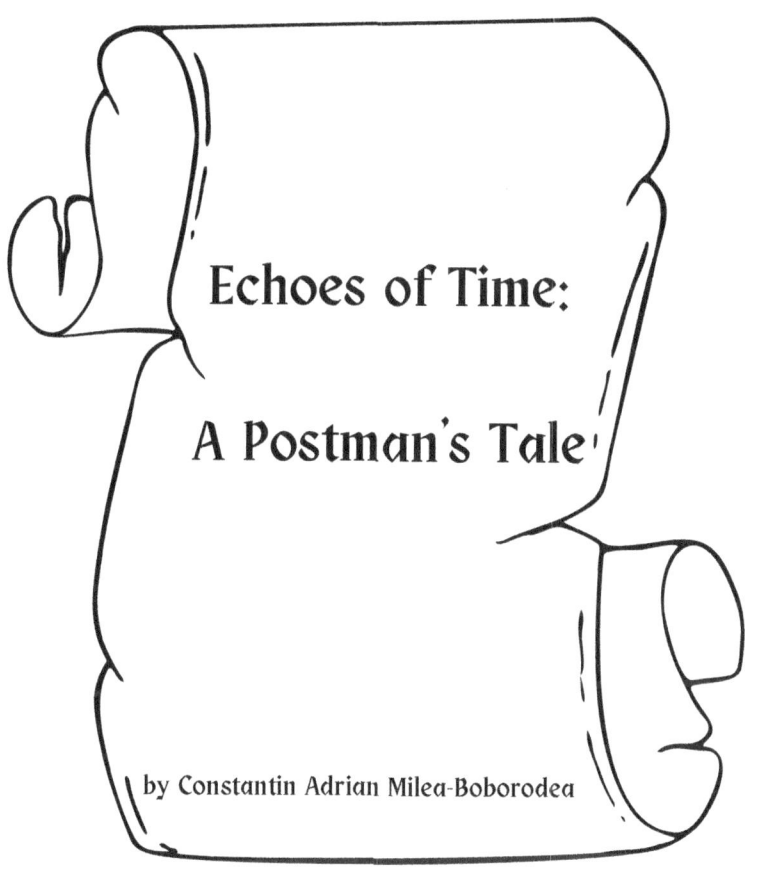

Echoes of Time:

A Postman's Tale

by Constantin Adrian Milea-Boborodea

Chapter 1: The Finding

Denver was a pleasant postman who lived in the quiet village of Ruyton XI Towns, surrounded by beautiful cottages and gently rolling hills. He was known for his punctuality and kind nature. At the village post office one misty morning, Denver was going through a stack of letters when he noticed a broken package that belonged to an elderly neighbour who had passed away.

From the damaged package a sleek, futuristic device fell right at Denver's feet. The gadget had flickering lights and a faint hum and was adorned with odd markings that put out an eerie shine. Denver, intrigued but not knowing what the item was , put it into his pocket with the intention to find out later.

Throughout the day, as he delivered letters to the villagers, Denver couldn't shake the feeling of excitement and curiosity about the mysterious device. Each house he visited seemed to hold a potential clue or a friendly face who might recognize the gadget.

As Denver continued his rounds, the device nestled securely in his coat pocket, he couldn't help but steal glances at it between delivering letters. Its smooth surface felt cool against his fingers whenever he touched it, and the soft hum it emitted seemed to whisper secrets only Denver could hear.At Mrs. Wilkins' cottage, an elderly lady known for her love of antiques and mysteries, Denver hesitated before delivering her letters.

Perhaps she would recognize this peculiar contraption. Mrs. Wilkins greeted Denver with a warm smile and a cup of tea, as she always did.Denver engaged in the chat after a while, talking about the weather and local news. "Mrs. Wilkins, I came across something today, something unusual.

"He retrieved the device from his pocket and placed it gently on the table between them. Mrs. Wilkins eyes widened with surprise as she examined it closely. "Why, Denver, this looks like nothing I've ever seen before," she remarked, her wrinkled fingers tracing the strange symbols carved on its surface."But it reminds me of a tale my grandmother once told me about a tourist who visited our village long ago."

According to Mrs. Wilkins, the tourist had spoken of distant lands and incredible inventions beyond anyone's imagination. Among the tourist's belongings was said to be a device much like the one Denver now held in his hands. "He claimed it could communicate across great distances," Mrs. Wilkins recounted, her voice tinged with wonder. "But he left in a hurry, and no one ever saw him or his gadget again." Denver listened carefully, captivated by the story. Could this device be the very same one from Mrs. Wilkins grandmother's tale?

The mystery deepened, and with each passing moment, Denver felt a surge of determination to uncover its secrets. After bidding Mrs. Wilkins goodbye and promising to keep her updated , Denver resumed his deliveries, his mind racing with questions.Who had sent this device to the old resident? Why it arrived now, after so many years? And most importantly, what was its purpose?

As he approached the village square, where the ancient oak tree stood sentinel over the cobblestone paths, Denver noticed a group of children playing nearby. With a sudden inspiration, he decided to show them the mysterious gadget. Children, after all, had a way for imagining the extraordinary.

"Hey kids, come over here for a moment," Denver called out, his voice carrying across the square. The children, curious and eager, gathered around as Denver revealed the device once more. Their eyes widened in awe at the sight of its blinking lights and enigmatic symbols.

"Do any of you recognize this?" Denver asked, kneeling down to their level. The children exchanged excited whispers, pointing out similarities to their favorite stories of magic and adventure. One brave soul, Tommy, ventured forth and tentatively touched the device. "Maybe it's a magic compass," he suggested with a grin. Denver chuckled, encouraged by their enthusiasm. "It could be," he agreed, his mind buzzing with possibilities. Perhaps these children held the key to unlocking the mystery of the device.

With renewed purpose, Denver continued on his rounds, now accompanied by a sense of shared excitement with the villagers and the children. Each stop brought new theories, old tales, and a growing sense of anticipation for what lay ahead. Little did Denver know that this discovery would not only change his life but also the fate of Ruyton XI Towns forever.

Chapter 2: The Enigma Unfolds

That evening, after finishing his rounds, Denver returned to his modest cottage on the outskirts of the village. Settling into his worn armchair by the fireplace, he carefully took out the device from his pocket and placed it on the wooden coffee table before him. The device glinted in the warm glow of the fire , its sleek surface reflecting the dancing flames.

With a mix of caution and fascination, Denver began to examine the device more closely. Its surface was smooth to the touch, decorated with intricate patterns and tiny buttons that seemed to respond to his slightest touch. He wondered if it was some kind of advanced communication device or perhaps a prototype from a tech-savvy resident who had moved away without a trace.

As Denver turned the device over in his hands, a faint whirring sound emanated from within, and suddenly, a beam of light shot out from its center , covering Denver in a swirling vortex of energy. The room spun around him, and in the blink of an eye, Denver found himself standing in a vastly different landscape.

The air around Denver crackled with unfamiliar energy as he blinked, trying to make sense of his surroundings.

Gone was his cosy cottage and the crackling fireplace; instead, he stood amidst towering crystalline structures that shimmered with a soft, supernatural glow. The ground beneath his feet felt strangely solid yet lowered slightly with each step, like walking on firm clouds.Denver's heart raced with a mixture of awe and confusion. Where had the device taken him? Was this another world altogether, or perhaps a distant corner of his own?

The landscape stretched out before him in shades of iridescent blues and purples, with distant shapes that resembled trees but glowed with a pulsating light.

As he cautiously explored this surreal terrain, Denver noticed movement in the periphery of his vision. Small, winged creatures dancing among the crystalline formations, emitting musical chirps that echoed softly through the air. They seemed curious about Denver, hovering at a distance but never approaching too closely.

Despite his initial shock, Denver's natural curiosity and sense of adventure took over. He tentatively reached out to touch one of the crystalline structures, marveling at its smooth, cool surface. It was unlike anything he had ever encountered in Ruyton XI Towns, or anywhere else for that matter.Just as he was beginning to acclimate to this strange new environment, a voice echoed in his mind—a gentle, melodious voice that seemed to resonate from the very air around him.

"Welcome, traveller" the voice said, its tone soothing yet tinged with mystery. "You have unlocked the gateway to the realm of Quoriana. Quoriana. The name sent shivers down Denver's spine. He had never heard of such a place in all his years of delivering mail and listening to villagers' tales.

 Yet here he stood, a humble postman from Ruyton XI Towns, on the threshold of an extraordinary world.

The voice continued, guiding Denver with instructions on how to navigate through Quoriana safely. It explained that the device he held was indeed a communication tool, capable of not only moving through physical distances but also bridging the gaps between realms. It had been left behind by a long-forgotten traveller who had stumbled upon Quoriana centuries ago.As Denver absorbed this revelation, he felt a surge of gratitude towards Mrs. Wilkins and the children who had sparked his journey earlier that day.

Their stories and imaginations had unknowingly prepared him for this unforeseen adventure. With newfound determination, Denver decided to explore Quoriana further, to uncover its secrets and perhaps find answers to questions he hadn't even thought to ask. The creatures around him seemed to sense his curiosity , their chirps becoming more melodious as if welcoming him to their realm.

But even as Denver embraced the wonder of Quoriana, a nagging thought tugged at the back of his mind—how would he return home? Was there a way back through the same vortex that had brought him here, or was his fate now connected with this mysterious realm?As he pondered these questions, Denver glanced back at the device resting on the ground beside him, its lights blinking softly in response to his presence. It seemed to pulse with a quiet reassurance, as if promising that all would become clear in time.

With a deep breath and a renewed sense of adventure, Denver took his first step into the heart of Quoriana, ready to uncover the enigma that awaited him and to embrace the unexpected journey that had unfolded from a simple discovery in his peaceful village.

Chapter 3: A Leap Through Time

Gone were the cosy comforts of his cottage and
the familiar sights of Ruyton XI Towns. Instead,
Denver found himself amidst the ruins of a grand
castle, surrounded by the clamour of battle. The
air was thick with the acrid smell of smoke and
the metallic tang of blood. Soldiers clad in chain
mail clashed with rebels wielding crude weapons,
their shouts echoing off the crumbling stone walls.
Discombobulated, Denver realised he had been
transported back in time to the year 1212, during
a pivotal battle between Welsh rebels and English
soldiers defending the castle. The scene before him
was chaotic and violent, a stark contrast to the
tranquil village life he knew. Naturally , Denver
sought cover behind a fallen pillar as arrows
whizzed overhead and swords clashed nearby.
He struggled to make sense of his surroundings,
his mind racing with questions about how he had
come to be in this dangerous situation and how he
could possibly return home.

As Denver crouched behind a fallen pillar, trying to shield himself from the chaos unfolding around him, his thoughts raced. The castle, once majestic and formidable, now stood battered and besieged. Flames licked at the edges of crumbling walls, casting flickering shadows that danced eerily across the courtyard.

Surrounded by the clash of swords and the cries of battle, Denver caught sight of figures heaved in heated combat. English soldiers, their armour gleaming dully in the dim light, fought with grim determination against Welsh rebels clad in ragged tunics and wielding weapons hastily crafted from wood and metal. The rebels moved with a fierce intensity, their faces contorted with both desperation and defiance.

As Denver watched, a surge of adrenaline coursed through him. He was keenly aware of the weight of the device tucked securely in his pocket, a stark reminder of the inexplicable journey that had brought him here.

How had he leaped through time from the fantastical realm of Quoriana to this brutal moment in history?

The air around him crackled with tension as he realized the gravity of his situation. One wrong move could mean disaster—caught between warring factions in a time not his own, with no clear path back to the peaceful village he had left behind.

A sudden movement caught Denver's eye—a young boy, no older than fourteen, stumbled past him with a wounded arm, clutching a makeshift dagger in his trembling hand. Their eyes met briefly, conveying a silent plea for help amid the chaos. Denver's heart went out to the boy, a strong reminder of the human cost of this conflict. Determined to find a way back home, Denver knew he needed to navigate this treacherous landscape with caution. The device, he realised, must hold the key not only to his return but perhaps to understanding the mysterious forces at play—both in Quoriana and in this tumultuous moment in history.

Summoning courage, Denver cautiously moved from his hiding place, keeping low to avoid drawing attention. His footsteps echoed faintly against the ancient stones as he edged closer to the fray, his senses sharp and alert for any sign of danger. He had to find a way to use the device, to harness its power to bend time and space once more.

As he reached a less crowded corner of the courtyard, Denver retrieved the device from his pocket, its lights pulsing softly in response to his touch. With trembling fingers, he pressed a sequence of buttons, hoping against hope that it would reactivate the mysterious portal that had transported him here.

The air seemed to shimmer for a moment, and Denver held his breath, willing the device to work its magic once more. But instead of another swirling vortex, there was only silence—a cold, unforgiving silence that left Denver feeling more alone than ever. Frustration gnawed at him as he realised the device was inert, its power momentarily depleted or perhaps attuned to forces beyond his understanding.Yet amidst the chaos and uncertainty, Denver refused to give up hope.There had to be another way, another path back to the village and the life he had known.

As he pondered his next move, a shout rang out from behind him, followed by the thunderous sound of hooves approaching at full gallop. Denver whirled around just in time to see a mounted knight bearing down upon him, lance leveled and visor gleaming menacingly in the firelight.

Instinct took over as Denver leaped to the side, narrowly avoiding the deadly charge. He jumped to his feet, heart pounding, desperately seeking refuge amidst the labyrinthine ruins of the castle. Every corner seemed to conceal new dangers, every shadow a potential threat.

But amid the chaos and peril, Denver's determination remained unbroken. He would find a way back home, he vowed, even if it meant braving the dangers of this unfamiliar time and place. With the device clutched tightly in his hand, he forged onward, guided by determination and the flickering hope that somewhere, somehow, a path would open—a path leading back to Ruyton XI Towns and the peaceful village life that now seemed so distant, yet achingly close.

Chapter 4: The Castle's Secrets

As Denver cautiously navigated through the chaos of battle, he realized that the castle was more than just a battleground—it held a dark secret coveted by both the Welsh rebels and the English garrison. Rumours whispered of a hidden treasure buried deep within the castle's labyrinthine tunnels, a treasure that could turn the tide of war in favour of whoever possessed it.

Driven by a mix of fear and determination, Denver ventured deeper into the castle, hoping to find answers that would lead him back to his own time. Along the way, he encountered allies and adversaries alike—a young squire named Thomas, who had dreams of knighthood despite his humble origins, and a grizzled English sergeant named Richard, who eyed Denver with suspicion but slowly accepted his presence.

Together, they navigated the treacherous corridors and shadowy chambers of the castle, evading patrols and uncovering clues about the mysterious device that had brought Denver here. It became clear that the device was not just a random gadget but a piece of advanced technology left behind by a secretive group of time travellers who sought to manipulate history for their own ends.

Denver, Thomas, and Richard made their way through a hidden passage that Thomas had discovered as a child.

The narrow tunnel was damp and cold, with water dripping from the ceiling and echoing through the stone walls. As they progressed, Denver couldn't shake the feeling that they were being watched. The hairs on the back of his neck stood on end, and he tightened his grip on the device.

After what felt like an eternity, they emerged into a vast underground chamber.

The walls were lined with ancient carvings depicting scenes of battles, triumphs, and mysterious figures holding devices similar to the one Denver possessed.In the center of the room, a massive stone door stood, covered in intricate symbols that glowed faintly in the dim light.

"This must be it." Thomas whispered, his voice filled with awe. "The entrance to the treasure."

Richard grunted, his eyes scanning the room for any signs of danger. "Let's not get ahead of ourselves, lad. We still need to figure out how to open it."

Denver stepped forward, examining the symbols on the door. They seemed to resonate with the device, their glow intensifying as he brought it closer. With a deep breath, he pressed the device against the door, and the symbols began to shift and rearrange themselves. Slowly, the stone door creaked open, revealing a hidden chamber beyond.

Inside, the treasure lay glittering in the torchlight—gold coins, gold crowns, and ancient artifacts that spoke of a time long forgotten.

But amid the riches, Denver's eyes were drawn to a pedestal in the center of the room.On it rested a small, intricately designed box that pulsed with a faint blue light.Thomas's eyes widened with excitement. "This is it! This is what we've been searching for!"

Richard, however, remained cautious. "Be careful, Denver. We don't know what that thing is or what it can do."Denver approached the pedestal, his heart pounding in his chest. As he reached out to touch the box, a sudden gust of wind swept through the chamber, extinguishing the torches and plunging them into darkness. The ground trembled beneath their feet, and a low, ominous rumble echoed through the tunnels. "What's happening?" Thomas shouted, panic creeping into his voice.

Denver grasped the box and the device in his hands, feeling a surge of energy course through him. The box seemed to respond to his touch, its blue light intensifying and casting eerie shadows on the walls.

He realised that the box and the device were connected, part of the same advanced technology that had brought him to this time. "We need to get out of here!" Denver yelled, trying to steady his voice. "I think the device is reacting to the box. It might be our way out!"

Richard and Thomas didn't need any further encouragement. They bolted for the tunnel, with Denver close behind, clutching the box tightly. As they raced through the darkened passages, the castle continued to shake, and the sound of collapsing stone echoed ominously around them. Emerging back into the courtyard, they were met with the chaotic sights and sounds of battle still raging.

Chapter 5: Trials and Tribulations

As days turned into weeks, Denver found himself caught in a relentless cycle of skirmishes, espionage, and desperate attempts to understand the device's capabilities. He learned to wield a sword and defend himself against foes who saw him as either a threat or a potential ally. Battles raged both within and outside the castle walls, each clash bringing Denver closer to unraveling the castle's secrets and finding a way back home. Amidst the turmoil, Denver forged bonds with unexpected allies—a resilient healer named Anna who tended to wounded soldiers regardless of their allegiance, and a cunning Welsh scout named Rhys who saw potential in Denver's knowledge of future warfare tactics. Together, they formed a fragile alliance, united by their shared goal of survival and discovery.

Anna, with her gentle way and constant dedication, became a beacon of hope for Denver. She possessed an uncanny ability to heal not just physical wounds but also the emotional scars of war.

Her skills were unmatched, and she carried herself with a quiet strength that inspired those around her. Denver often found solace in her presence, discussing the mysteries of the device and the strange journey that had brought him to this time. Anna, in turn, shared stories of her own struggles and the resilience of the human spirit.

Rhys, on the other hand, was a master of stealth and strategy. His knowledge of the Welsh terrain and guerrilla tactics proved invaluable in their efforts to evade both English and rebel forces. Rhys admired Denver's ingenuity and willingness to adapt, often drawing on Denver's insights from the future to plan daring raids and ambushes.
 In return, Denver learned from Rhys the art of survival in a hostile environment, the importance of trust, and the value of loyalty.

Together, they navigated the treacherous corridors and shadowy chambers of the castle, evading patrols and uncovering clues about the mysterious device that had brought Denver here. It became clear that the device was not just a random gadget but a piece of advanced technology left behind by a secretive group of time travellers who sought to manipulate history for their own ends.

However, danger lurked at every turn. Denver faced betrayal from within his own ranks and narrowly escaped capture by Welsh raiding parties intent on uncovering the castle's hidden treasure. Each close call tested his courage and resolve, reminding him of the stakes involved in meddling with the fabric of time itself.

One night, as Denver sat by the fire in a hidden chamber beneath the castle, Anna approached him with a look of determination. "Denver, we need to talk," she said, her voice steady but urgent.

Denver nodded, sensing the gravity of her words. "What is it, Anna?"

"I've been thinking about the device," she began, "and I believe it holds the key to not only your return home but also to ending this war. If we can harness its power, we might be able to alter the course of history and bring peace to our lands." Rhys, who had been listening intently, chimed in. "She's right, Denver. We need to understand how it works and use it to our advantage. But we must be careful. There are those who would stop at nothing to seize it for themselves."

Denver knew they were right. The device was a double-edged sword, capable of immense power but fraught with danger. They needed to unlock its secrets and protect it from falling into the wrong hands. "Alright," he agreed, determination hardening his voice. "Let's figure this out together."

Their first step was to decode the symbols and patterns on the device. Anna, with her keen eye for detail, meticulously documented each symbol, comparing them to ancient texts and scrolls hidden within the castle's library.

Rhys used his network of spies and informants to gather intelligence on the movements of both English and Welsh forces, ensuring they stayed one step ahead of their enemies.

Denver, meanwhile, focused on experimenting with the device, cautiously pressing its buttons and observing its reactions. He discovered that the device responded to specific sequences, each combination triggering a different function. Some sequences emitted beams of light that revealed hidden passages, while others produced sounds that echoed through the castle's walls, hinting at unseen mechanisms.

Days turned into nights as they worked tirelessly, their efforts finally yielding results. They uncovered a hidden chamber deep within the castle, a vault that had remained untouched for centuries. Inside, they found ancient manuscripts and artifacts, evidence of the time travellers presence in this era.

The manuscripts contained detailed instructions on how to operate the device, along with warnings about the consequences of tampering with time. Armed with this newfound knowledge, Denver, Anna, and Rhys devised a plan.

They would use the device to create a temporary truce between the warring factions, presenting themselves as emissaries of a powerful force capable of altering the course of history. With luck, they could broker peace and avert further bloodshed.

But as they prepared to put their plan into action, betrayal struck from within. A trusted member of their group, tempted by the promise of power and riches, revealed their plans to a rival faction. Denver, Anna, and Rhys found themselves ambushed in the dead of night, their sanctuary compromised.

In the chaos that ensued, Denver fought valiantly, wielding his newfound skills with precision. Rhys, ever the strategist, orchestrated their escape, leading them through hidden tunnels and secret passages. Anna tended to the wounded, her hands steady despite the turmoil around her.

.

As they regrouped in a secluded glen outside the castle, Denver realised the gravity of their situation they were no longer just fighting for their own survival but for the fate of their world. The device was a powerful tool, and its potential for both good and evil was immense.

With renewed resolve, they pressed on, determined to see their mission through to the end. The trials and tribulations they faced only strengthened their bond, forging them into an unbreakable team. And as the final battle loomed on the horizon, Denver knew that their journey was far from over.

Together, they would face whatever challenges lay ahead, armed with courage, knowledge, and the hope that they could change the course of history for the better. And with the device in hand, they would unlock the secrets of time and find a way back to the world they had left behind, forever changed by the trials they had endured.

Chapter 6: The Manipulators of Time

As Denver delved deeper into the mysteries of the castle and the secrets it held, he uncovered disturbing truths about the time-travel device and the group of manipulators who sought to alter history for their own gain. They were led by a shadowy figure known only as the Watcher, a master of temporal manipulation who saw the past as a canvas to be reshaped according to his whims.

Denver's investigation began in earnest, piecing together clues from ancient manuscripts and cryptic symbols scattered throughout the castle. The castle's library, filled with dusty tomes and forgotten scrolls, became his sanctuary. There, he discovered records of strange events that had occurred over the centuries—events that could only be explained by the presence of time travellers. Each incident bore the mark of the Watcher, a symbol resembling an eye, ominously watching over history.

One evening, as Denver pored over an ancient map of the castle, he found a hidden compartment within the library's walls. Inside, he uncovered a journal written by a former inhabitant of the castle, a scholar named Eadric, who had stumbled upon the Watcher's manipulations centuries ago. Eadric's journal detailed his attempts to thwart the Watcher, but it ended abruptly, leaving Denver to wonder about the scholar's fate.

Confronted with the consequences of the Watcher's actions, Denver realized that the fate of both past and present lay in his hands. He couldn't simply return home and leave the castle and its inhabitants to their fate. Determined to set things right, Denver rallied his allies and devised a plan to confront the manipulators and reclaim the time-travel device.

Gathering Anna, Rhys, Thomas, and Richard in a secret chamber, Denver shared his findings. "We are not just fighting for ourselves," he declared. "We are fighting for the integrity of history itself.

The Watcher and his followers have been altering events to suit their needs, and if we don't stop them, the consequences could be catastrophic."

Anna nodded, her expression resolute. "We must act quickly and decisively. But how do we find the Watcher and his followers?"

Rhys stepped forward, a determined glint in his eyes. "I've been tracking their movements. There's an old tower on the outskirts of the castle grounds. It's heavily guarded, but I believe it's where they're operating from."

Denver looked at his allies, their faces a mix of fear and determination. "We need to move under the cover of darkness. Rhys, lead the way. Anna, prepare whatever healing supplies you can. Richard, Thomas, make sure our weapons are ready. We must be prepared for anything."

As night fell, the group set out for the tower. The castle grounds were eerily silent, the air thick with anticipation. Rhys led them through hidden pathways and overgrown trails, his knowledge of the terrain proving invaluable.

When they reached the tower, they found it surrounded by guards, their armour glinting in the moonlight.

"What's the plan, Denver?" Richard whispered, his hand resting on the hilt of his sword.

"We need to create a diversion," Denver replied. "Rhys, can you lead a small group to draw the guards away? The rest of us will use that distraction to infiltrate the tower."

Rhys nodded. "Consider it done."

With a silent signal, Rhys and a few handpicked men disappeared into the shadows. Moments later, the sound of clashing steel and shouted orders echoed through the night. The guards around the tower rushed towards the commotion, leaving their posts unguarded.

"Now's our chance," Denver whispered. "Let's move."

They slipped through the shadows, reaching the tower's entrance undetected. Inside, the air was thick with the scent of burning incense and the hum of strange machinery.

Denver led the way, his heart pounding as they ascended the spiral staircase, each step bringing them closer to the Watcher.

At the top of the tower, they found a grand chamber filled with arcane devices and ancient relics. The Watcher stood at the center, a tall figure cloaked in dark robes, his face obscured by a hood. He turned to face them, his eyes gleaming with a cold, calculating light.

"Ah, Denver," the Watcher said, his voice a low, mocking tone. "I've been expecting you."

Denver stepped forward, his grip tightening on the device. "Your manipulations end here, Watcher. You can't play with history for your own gain."

The Watcher chuckled softly. "You are naive, Denver. History is malleable, a tool to be shaped by those with the vision to see its true potential."

Anna stepped forward, her voice steady and strong. "You have no right to decide the fate of countless lives. We will stop you."

The Watcher's smile faded, replaced by a look of disdain.

"You think you can stop me? You are but ants, scurrying about in a world you barely comprehend."

With a swift motion, the Watcher activated a control panel on the device. The room filled with a blinding light, and Denver felt the ground shift beneath his feet. When the light faded, they found themselves standing in a vast, desolate landscape, the castle and its surroundings replaced by a barren wasteland.

"What have you done?" Denver demanded, his voice echoing in the emptiness.

The Watcher laughed, a harsh, mirthless sound. "Welcome to the future you have fought so hard to protect. A future where my vision prevails."

Denver felt a surge of determination. "This isn't over, Watcher. We will find a way to undo this."

With renewed resolve, Denver and his allies faced the daunting task ahead. They were in a race against time itself, battling not just for their survival but for the fate of history.

The manipulations of the Watcher and his followers had brought them to the brink, but Denver knew that they had the strength and determination to set things right.

Together, they would confront the Watcher and his forces, armed with knowledge, courage, and the hope that they could restore the timeline and find their way back home. The journey ahead was fraught with danger, but Denver was ready to face whatever trials awaited them, knowing that the fate of the past, present, and future rested in their hands.

Chapter 7: The Final Confrontation

The castle's courtyard was a scene of chaos as
Denver and his allies prepared for the climactic
showdown against the Watcher and his cohorts.
The air was thick with an acrid smell and a
deafening roar . Shadows danced wildly across the
crumbling stone walls as flames licked the night
sky, casting an eerie glow over the battleground.
Denver, his heart pounding with a mix of fear and
determination, gathered his closest allies—Anna,
Rhys, Thomas, and Richard—at the entrance to
the castle's keep. "This is it," he said, his voice
steady despite the turmoil. "We must take down
the Watcher and his followers. They cannot be
allowed to manipulate history any longer."
Anna nodded, her eyes fierce with resolve. "We'll
follow your lead, Denver. Let's end this."
As they charged into the keep, the battle
intensified.

Denver's knowledge of future warfare tactics proved invaluable as he directed his allies, coordinating their movements with precision. Rhys led a group of archers to higher ground, their arrows raining down on the Watcher's soldiers. Thomas and Richard, swords in hand, fought valiantly alongside Denver, cutting through enemy lines with a determination born of desperation.

In the heart of the castle, Denver spotted the Watcher, surrounded by his loyalists. The shadowy figure's eyes gleamed with malevolent intent, his presence commanding and sinister. Denver knew that this was the moment they had been preparing for—the final confrontation that would determine the fate of history itself.

"Anna, we need to get to the device," Denver shouted over the din of battle. "It's the only way to stop him."

Anna nodded, her face set with determination. "Let's go."

As they made their way through the chaos, alliances shifted and betrayals unfolded. One of their supposed allies, lured by the promise of power, turned against them, attacking Richard from behind. Richard, though wounded, managed to fend off the traitor, but the betrayal left them shaken.

"We have to keep moving," Denver urged, helping Richard to his feet. "We can't let them stop us now."

Finally, they reached the grand hall where the time-travel device was housed. The Watcher stood before it, his dark robes billowing like shadows come to life. "You are too late, Denver," he sneered. "History is mine to control."

Denver stepped forward, his sword raised. "Not if I can help it."

The battle that ensued was fierce and chaotic. Denver and the Watcher clashed in a flurry of steel and sparks, their swords ringing out as they fought for control of the device.

Around them, their allies engaged the Watcher's loyalists, the clash of swords creating a cacophony of sound.

As the fight raged on, Anna managed to reach the device. She studied its controls, her fingers deftly pressing buttons and turning dials. "Denver, I think I can activate it," she called out, her voice tinged with urgency.

The Watcher, realizing his defeat was imminent, lunged at Anna. Denver intercepted him, their swords locking in a deadly embrace. "You won't win," Denver gritted out, pushing the Watcher back.

With a final, desperate surge of strength, Denver disarmed the Watcher and sent him sprawling to the ground. "Now, Anna!" he shouted.

Anna pressed the final sequence of buttons, and the device began to hum with power. A bright light enveloped the room, and the ground beneath them trembled. Jack and his allies held their breath, hoping that Anna's efforts would succeed.

As the light grew blindingly bright, Denver felt a sudden shift. The room around them seemed to warp and distort, the very fabric of reality bending to the device's power. When the light finally faded, they found themselves back in the castle's courtyard, but the flames and chaos were gone. The battle had never taken place.

Denver looked around, his heart pounding. "Did it work?" he asked, his voice barely above a whisper.

Anna nodded, her face alight with relief. "I think so. We've undone the Watcher's manipulations. History should be restored."

As they stood there, the castle's inhabitants began to emerge from their hiding places, confused but unharmed. The timeline had been corrected, and the damage caused by the Watcher and his followers had been erased.

Denver, Anna, Rhys, Thomas, and Richard stood together, a sense of victory and relief washing over them. "We did it," Denver said, his voice filled with awe. "We actually did it."

But as the dust settled, Denver knew that their journey was not over. The time-travel device had been used to undo the Watcher's damage, but its power remained a dangerous temptation. They needed to ensure it was protected, its secrets kept safe from those who would misuse it.

"Now we need to make sure this never happens again," Denver said, his resolve firm. "The device must be hidden, its secrets buried."

His allies nodded in agreement, understanding the gravity of their task. Together, they would protect the device and safeguard history, ensuring that the past, present, and future remained free from the manipulations of those who sought to control time.As they began the work of securing the device and rebuilding their lives, Denver felt a sense of peace. They had faced unimaginable challenges and emerged victorious, their bonds forged in the crucible of battle. And though their journey had been fraught with trials, they had proven that courage, determination, and the strength of their friendship could overcome even the most daunting of obstacles.

Chapter 8: The Return Home

With a blinding flash of light, Denver found himself back in the familiar streets of Ruyton XI Towns. The device lay inert in his hand, its purpose fulfilled. The early morning sun cast long shadows across the cobblestone streets, and the village stirred with the beginnings of a new day. Birds chirped in the hedgerows, and the distant sound of sheep bleating on the hills brought a sense of serene normalcy.

Exhausted yet exhilarated, Denver felt the weight of the device in his pocket—a relic of his extraordinary journey. He looked around, half expecting the world to have changed, but everything seemed as it always was. The stone cottages with their thatched roofs stood just as they had before, and the villagers went about their daily routines, blissfully unaware of the epic adventure that had unfolded.

Denver returned to his modest cottage on the outskirts of the village, the same worn armchair by the fireplace greeting him as he entered. Sitting down heavily, he took a deep breath, feeling the enormity of his experiences settle upon him. He carefully placed the device in a small, ornate box and tucked it away in a hidden compartment under the floorboards. It was a secret he intended to keep, a powerful reminder of the past and a safeguard for the future.

In the days that followed, Denver resumed his role as the village postman. The routine of sorting letters and delivering letters provided a comforting rhythm, a stark contrast to the chaos and danger he had faced. However, he found himself viewing his surroundings with new eyes. The simple act of handing a letter to Mrs. Wilkins or chatting with old Mr. Thompson about the weather held a deeper significance. He had come to understand the profound impact of every moment and every choice, the delicate threads that wove the tapestry of history.

Though he never spoke of his adventures to the villagers, Denver carried with him the lessons he had learned about courage, loyalty, and the consequences of tampering with time. His journey had not just been a battle against an enemy but a discovery of inner strength and the power of unity. He had forged bonds with people from different eras and backgrounds, and these experiences had reshaped his perspective on life and history.

One evening, as the sun set over the rolling hills, Denver found himself reflecting on the friends he had made—Anna, Rhys, Thomas, and Richard. He wondered about their fates in the corrected timeline, hoping that their lives had found peace and fulfillment. The memories of their shared struggles and victories warmed his heart, reminding him of the indomitable human spirit. Denver's encounters with the villagers took on new meaning. He listened more intently to their stories, appreciating the rich tapestry of experiences that each person contributed to the collective history of Ruyton XI Towns.

He found joy in the mundane, from the laughter of children playing in the streets to the vibrant colours of the market stalls. The village was a living chronicle, and Denver felt honored to be a part of it.

And as he delivered mail each day, Denver couldn't help but smile, knowing that beneath the tranquil surface of his village lay a history rich with untold stories and secrets waiting to be discovered.

The device remained safely hidden away, a silent guardian of time's mysteries. Denver understood the responsibility he bore in keeping it secret and safe, a custodian of the past and a protector of the future.

In quiet moments, Denver would often gaze at the horizon, contemplating the infinite possibilities of time and the remarkable journey that had brought him back home. He felt a profound sense of gratitude for the life he had, the people he knew, and the village he loved.

For Denver, the past was no longer a distant memory but a living, breathing entity that shaped the present and guided the future.

And so, Denver lived out his days in Ruyton XI Towns, a humble postman with an extraordinary secret. His adventures had ended, but the lessons he had learned continued to resonate, a testament to the resilience of the human spirit and the enduring power of time.

Chapter 9: The Unending Loop

Denver's return to the peaceful routine of Ruyton XI Towns was a welcome respite from the chaos and danger he had faced in the past. He resumed his daily rounds with a renewed appreciation for the simple life, grateful to be back among familiar faces and places.

The following day, Denver awoke to the gentle sounds of birds chirping outside his window. The sun's rays filtered through the curtains, casting a warm glow over his modest cottage. He dressed in his familiar postman's uniform and headed to the village post office to begin his rounds.As Denver sorted through the day's letters, he came across a package that looked eerily familiar. His heart skipped a beat as he noticed the damaged parcel, its contents barely concealed by the torn wrapping. He cautiously opened it and, to his astonishment, found the same sleek, futuristic device with blinking lights and strange symbols that had started his extraordinary journey.

For a moment, Denver stood frozen, his mind racing with the implications of this discovery. The device seemed to hum softly, as if recognizing him and beckoning him to use it once more. He knew that activating it could plunge him back into the past, into the heart of a medieval conflict and the clutches of those who sought to alter history. With a deep breath, Denver slipped the device into his pocket, resolving to investigate its origins and purpose further.

As he continued his rounds, the weight of the device felt heavier with each step, a constant reminder of the extraordinary events he had experienced and the potential for more adventures to come.

Chapter 10: A New Adventure Begins

That evening, as Denver sat by the fireplace, the device's glow cast dancing shadows on the walls. He knew that he couldn't ignore its presence, nor could he dismiss the possibility that his journey through time was far from over. Determined to uncover the truth, Denver decided to consult the few villagers who might possess knowledge of such mysterious artifacts.

He visited the village historian, an elderly woman named Margaret, whose extensive knowledge of local legends and lore might hold clues about the device. Margaret listened intently as Denver recounted his story, her eyes widening with each revelation. She revealed that ancient texts spoke of a powerful artifact capable of traversing time, guarded by a secretive order known as the Chronomancers.

Intrigued and armed with this newfound information, Denver realized that his journey was only just beginning. The device, it seemed, was not merely a tool for travel but a key to unlocking deeper mysteries about the nature of time itself. Unable to resist the allure of discovery, Denver activated the device once more. The familiar beam of light enveloped him, and the world spun around him in a dizzying whirl of colours and sounds. When the light faded, he found himself back in the turbulent year of 1212, amidst the ruins of the castle where his previous adventure had taken place.

But this time, Denver was prepared. He sought out his old allies—Thomas, Anna, and the Welsh scout—and shared his knowledge of the Chronomancers and their intentions.

United by a common purpose, they embarked on a quest to uncover the secrets of the time-travel device and thwart the manipulative schemes of the Watcher and his cohorts.

As Denver navigated the treacherous landscape of medieval England once more, he realized that his journey was part of a larger, ongoing struggle to protect the integrity of history. The Chronomancers, the Watcher, and the device itself were all part of a complex web of events that transcended time and space.

Each battle, each alliance, and each discovery brought Denver closer to understanding his role in this grand narrative. He became a guardian of time, committed to ensuring that the past remained unaltered and the future safeguarded.

Epilogue: A Glimpse of Tomorrow

Back in the present day, Denver returned to his routine, delivering letters with the same dedication and care he always had. Yet, the device never left his thoughts, a constant reminder of the extraordinary power and responsibility it carried. Each day he wondered if the cycle would begin anew, if he would once again be called upon to protect the flow of time.

As Denver approached the village post office one sunny morning, a familiar sense of anticipation washed over him. He reached into the mailbox and pulled out a package, its damaged wrapping revealing a glimpse of the sleek, futuristic device within.

He smiled, a mixture of excitement and determination filling his heart. Denver knew that his adventures were far from over. The secrets of the Chronomancers awaited, and with them, new allies, enemies, and challenges beyond his imagination.

As he pocketed the device, ready for whatever lay ahead, Denver took a deep breath and continued his rounds, knowing that his destiny as a guardian of time was an endless journey, full of twists, turns, and infinite possibilities.

To Be Continued...

This narrative is a work of fiction. Although it draws on historical events, certain elements have been modified or enhanced for storytelling purposes.

Thank you!

Printed in Great Britain
by Amazon

45071426R00037